William John Courthope

The Paradise of Birds

An Old Extravaganza in a Modern Dress. Second Edition

William John Courthope

The Paradise of Birds
An Old Extravaganza in a Modern Dress. Second Edition

ISBN/EAN: 9783337207311

Printed in Europe, USA, Canada, Australia, Japan

Cover: Foto ©Andreas Hilbeck / pixelio.de

More available books at **www.hansebooks.com**

THE PARADISE OF BIRDS

AN OLD EXTRAVAGANZA IN A MODERN DRESS

BY

WILLIAM JOHN COURTHOPE

AUTHOR OF 'LUDIBRIA LUNÆ'

SECOND EDITION

" Rien n'est si joli que la fable, si triste que la vérité"

WILLIAM BLACKWOOD AND SONS
EDINBURGH AND LONDON
MDCCCLXXIII

I DEDICATE THESE PAGES TO

MY SISTER,

IN MEMORY OF THE BIRDS WHO SANG TO US BY

THE FIRST HOME OF OUR CHILDHOOD

THE SAME SONG THAT THEIR

CHILDREN'S CHILDREN ARE STILL REPEATING

IN THE BRANCHES.

DRAMATIS PERSONÆ.

MARESNEST, a Philosopher of the "Development" Persuasion.
WINDBAG, a Poet of the Romantic School.
BIRDCATCHER,
COOK, } Souls in Purgatory.
LADY,
ROC, an extinct Bird in his Egg-Shell, the Gate of Limbo.
BIRD OF PARADISE, King of the Birds' Paradise.
JACKDAW,
ROOK,
PIGEON,
LARK,
NIGHTINGALE,
GOLDFINCH, } Birds in Paradise.
BLACKBIRD,
THRUSH,
LINNET,
SWALLOW,
GOOSE,
CHORUS OF HUMAN BEINGS IN PURGATORY.
CHORUS OF EXTINCT BIRDS IN THE SHELL.
CHORUS OF BIRDS IN PARADISE.
A JURY OF TWELVE BIRDS.

Colle sub Elysio nigrâ nemus ilice frondens,
Udaque perpetuo gramine terra, viret.
Si qua fides dubiis vohierum locus ille piarum
Dicitur, obscenæ qua prohibentur aves."
—OVID, *Amorum*, l. ii. 6, 49.

Ἄγε δὴ φύσιν ἄνδρες ἀμαυρόβιοι, φύλλων γενεᾷ προσόμοιοι,
ὀλιγοδρανέες, πλάσματα πηλοῦ, σκιοειδέα φῦλ' ἀμενηνά,
ἀπτῆνες ἐφημέριοι, ταλαοι βροτοὶ, ἀνέρες εἰκελόνειροι,
πρόσχετε τὸν νοῦν τοῖς ἀθανάτοις ἡμῖν, τοῖς αἰὲν ἐοῦσι,
τοῖς αἰθερίοις, τοῖσιν ἀγήρως, τοῖς ἄφθιτα μηδομένοισιν,
ἵν' ἀκούσαντες πάντα παρ' ἡμῶν ὀρθῶς περὶ τῶν μετεώρων,
φύσιν οἰωνῶν, γένεσίν τε θεῶν, ποταμῶν τ' Ἐρέβους τε Χάους τε,
εἰδότες ὀρθῶς παρ' ἐμου Προδίκῳ κλάειν εἴπητε τὸ λοιπόν.

—ARISTOPHANES, *Aves*, 685.

THE PARADISE OF BIRDS.

Enter as Prologue, NIGHTINGALE.

NIGHTINGALE.

KIND gentlemen, and ladies dear,
To a poor nightingale give ear.
The poet bids me fly to you,
His audience fit (since doubtless few),
And introduce my bill of fare
For the entertainment we prepare.
If then you choose to taste the same,
And feel disgust—we're free from blame.
And first I say that, by your grace,
We mean to represent a place
To human sailors (save alone
To Fancy and her crew) unknown :

A

Not yet subjected to the reign
Of Science, tyrant and profane,—
The would-be queen, and upstart thief,
Who steals the lands of old Belief—
But unexplored (thank Heaven !) and free
To Wonder and to Poetry.

Strange things in this strange place you'll view ;
Conclude not therefore they're untrue.
Fancy of all things takes precedence
In travel,—so she should in credence :
For once 'twas fashion to traduce,
But now you all believe in, Bruce.
Besides, in this our moral age,
Bards have so serious grown and sage,
(Not to say dull), and all, forsooth,
Are so well paid for preaching Truth,
You might as soon suspect pretension
In priests, as poets of Invention.

Know, too, beforehand, that we birds
Shall speak with men in human words.
If such a prodigy displease,
Quarrel with Aristophanes :

Despise the light good-natured age
That clapped "the Birds" upon the stage ;
And yet what pleased the Athenian state,
England, methinks, might tolerate.

Critics, fastidious and select,
Hear what from me you must expect.
If you my friend and poet praise,
You shall be happy all your days.
I will come flying in the moon,
And sing to you each night in June ;
Restore the freshness to your brain,
When you have many authors slain,
And bring of epigrams a store,
That you may slay as many more.
But if this play you shall abuse,
Expect from all the feathered crews
Dire retribution.   I will rouse
Vast twittering armies in the boughs ;
(Nor deem your persons will to us
Be sacred, since anonymous)
Then, if your Sunday clothes you wear,
And walk abroad to take the air,
To preach or visit, dine or wed,—
Keep an umbrella overhead.

SCENE—*The Open Polar Sea.*

Enter on an iceberg, drawn by a hundred white bears,
WINDBAG *and* MARESNEST.

WINDBAG.

" Holloa ! you pampered jades of Greenland, heh !
What ! can you draw but twenty leagues a-day ? "
                                        (*Lashing the bears.*)
O how divine a thing is Poetry !
She gives men lordship over sea and sky ;
Dante to Hell descended by her boon ;
Through her bold Astolf mounted to the moon ;
And now, through Poetry, earth's wished-for goal
Lies within grasp :—She brings us to the Pole !
Who but a poet, even in hope, had sailed
Where all, though hopeful, have for ever failed ;
Some frozen helpless in the icy pack ;
Some by the snow-winds baffled and blown back ;

Some wasted by the long night's bitter air ;
And some worn out by fasting and despair?
Or, if another's boldness might essay,
What but a poet's wit had found a way?

MARESNEST.

Alas! dear Windbag, can you nothing spy?

WINDBAG.

Nothing but countless stars in sea and sky.

MARESNEST.

But not a bird? not even a curlew?

WINDBAG.

No.

By Mother Carey.

MARESNEST.

Do the waves not show
A single feather on their face?

WINDBAG.

Not one.

MARESNEST.

Now by the Pigeon, I am quite undone!
Seven days at sea! the Pole not yet appeared!
Woe's me! all stiff and crystal is my beard!
I am most straitly frozen to my hose,
Nor can I feel my fingers or my nose.
I seem an icicle threescore years old,
As sharp, as blue, as brittle, and as cold.
What if there were no Paradise indeed?

WINDBAG.

Oh! as to that all poets are agreed.
None doubt the Earthly Paradise a fact:
The knowledge of the site is less exact.
Far in the East it was of old professed;
Then moved to El-Dorado in the west;
Then backward to Cathay: but now at least
This much we know, 'tis neither west nor east.
Throughout our ample globe one spot alone
Is to the bold geographer unknown.
Here then our goal, all else discovered, lies;
Logic proclaims, the Pole is Paradise.

MARESNEST.

Well, grant the Paradise exists ; but then,
How prove you it is held by birds, not men ?

WINDBAG.

Man, who has made the others all his own,
Is still a stranger to the Arctic Zone.
Our species dwindle towards the ice and snow,
And speech is hushed beyond the Esquimaux.
High in the northern silence speechless things
Own the bare ice, and reign the Ocean's kings ;
Below, the seal, the fox, the Arctic bear,
And at the Pole itself the birds of air.

MARESNEST.

How then explain our wants ? what signs ? what words ?
Can speakers treat with speechless ? men with birds ?

WINDBAG.

My Maresnest, speech with mortals is the art
That veils the thoughts and secrets of the heart.

The Bird has thoughts like Man, but while they live,
Both to one feeling various utterance give.
Yet even in life the grammar of the tree
Was by our Chaucer learned, and Canace;
And, now the birds are dead, we at the Pole
Shall speak the common language of the soul.

MARESNEST.

Oh! had I never with this madman come,
But labelled shells and botanised at home!

WINDBAG.

Nay, never lose your courage, my good sir;
Let out your fancy, like a cockchafer
Tied by one leg : you will at once surmise
We are in regions hard by Paradise.
My breast breathes many a heavenly delight,
This to begin with—it is always night.
Now don't you see the beauty in it, pray?

MARESNEST.

Why, no, except that it is never day.

WINDBAG.

Is it then nought to have left our temperate clime,
With its old calendared and humdrum time,
Where the slow days in measured dulness run,
So much divided dark, and so much sun?
This silence, too,—O how unlike our shores,
Where with ten thousand tongues each city roars!
Where to all men, whate'er their age or walk,
Life's one great solemn business is to talk.
Where what the penny press by morning write,
Is echoed for a halfpenny at night;
Where stump young Ministers; old Maids debate;
Where loud Professors scold like Billingsgate;
Where, as the World into the Church expands,
A moral Atheist spouts in parson's bands;
And poets, doubtful of the parts of speech,
Desperate of rhyme, acquire the art to preach.
Here all is ruled by Silence, far and wide,
Save light waves lapping on the iceberg's side;
The moon laughs mutely o'er the watery space;
Each star shines down a still ironic face;
All nature lies inhuman, voiceless, bright;
"Vive le Silence!" say I; "Long live the Night!"

MARESNEST.

O for a thousand minstrels of all lands,
Waits, ballad-singers, organs, bones, brass bands,
Scotch bagpipes, squeaking fiddle, cracked bassoon,
Each shrieking out of time a different tune,
To shiver the still air with myriad jars,
Before I die of *ennui* and these stars !

WINDBAG.

How cowardly you talk !   We both are men.
Suppose the worst ; say we are lost ;—what then ?
We 'scape at least Oblivion's harder fate :
Hugo himself our story will relate.
How will he paint the great contrasted scene,
Our human agony, the heavens serene !
The iceberg glittering o'er the darksome tide !
And all we feared, felt, fancied, when we died !
Immortal monument !   The world will mock
At Valjean's sewer, and Gillyat on the rock.
Such polar winds in every thought will blow,
Each word a spasm, each full stop a throe ;
While, to close all, some huge stage-thunder phrase
Will make the simple gape, and Swinburne praise.

MARESNEST.

I do not like this fellow : in this light
I feel my blood mere zero Fahrenheit :
I shall go lower and avoid his sight.

(*Descends the iceberg.*)

Meantime, to explain the state of our affairs,
Both of ourselves, our iceberg, and our bears,
Which seem perhaps unusual.   Know then,
O lovely ladies, courteous gentlemen,
We who appear in this outlandish place,
In times so dark, in such prodigious case,
That from some star you might suppose us hurled,
Are human bipeds, citizens of the World,
In which Republic, I would have you know it,
I am a Naturalist, and he a Poet.
Hither we sail amid these icy blocks,
Full of philanthropy and paradox,
To benefit our species : in brief words,
We've come to make a treaty with the Birds.
Next for the cause ;—but first, to make things clear,
You should my theory of existence hear,
Learn all the worth of Man, and who you are,
That we have ventured for your sakes so far.

Two vital instincts spring in every brood.
Desire of children, and demand for food.
Children, as by the census is confessed,
Increase each year at compound interest;
But food's like barren capital, a store
Fit to support so many, and no more.
Hence betwixt animals arises strife;
The strong invades his neighbour's means of life;
The feeble neighbour, starved of his supplies,
Gets feebler sons; at last the species dies.
(The Bulls and Bears by instance may explain—
The race that battens on the public brain:
When money floats, and all the world blows bubbles,
This tribe lives friendly, propagates, and doubles;
But when the public folly spends its air,
The hungry Bull exterminates the Bear.)
So die the weak: the stronger, who survive,
Emerge more fair, and by extinction thrive;
Elect fit mates, and so improve their race,
Acquire variety, develop grace;
And, conqueror still of every conquering clan,
The first (till lately) in this strife was Man.
Hopeful and bold, progressive from his birth,
Man through all quarters of productive earth

Advanced his posts : he sowed the shore with crops,
Turned mountain-summits into turnip-tops,
Cut down the virginal forests, drove a share
O'er barren waves, and tracked the pathless air.
Where'er he made his dwelling, far and wide
The ancient speechless tenants pined and died ;
First the wild beasts, and then the gentler herds
Of antlered game, and last of all the Birds.
These, by the new-built town from woodlands chased,
Soon proved attractive to the city taste.
The truant schoolboy sought their mossy nests ;
The milliner their plumes and curving breasts.
Others, preferred from their Seven-Dials court,
Made for the gentler Gun Club generous sport ;
While cooks and beauties claimed an even share—
Cooks for their pies, and beauties for their hair.
In short, by such proscription, one by one,
Cut off to improve man's cookery, clothes, or gun,
The holiday of birds is most distinctly done.
No swallows skim our pools ; no wagtail's seen
The dainty-stepping Duchess of the green ;
Walk a long day in June through cherries ripe,
But never hope to hear a blackbird pipe.
Who loves at eve the home-returning rooks,

Who monkish daws, remote in cloistered nooks,
Who the light owl, with great white wings outspread,
He loves in vain—for all the birds are dead !
If it were well that lives so bright and gay
Should thus be quenched, is not for me to say :
Men are progressive animals :—but hear
From this extinction what results appear.
The Birds being gone, the Caterpillars, freed
From all restraints, began to enlarge their breed.
The chaffer in the wheat his larvæ laid ;
Dark weevils, mustering like the Cossack, preyed
Upon each leaf, and blackened every blade.
Scorched up, as though by arson, sword, or plague,
Our land lies sickening through every league ;
Our children pine beneath the wingèd curse,
Our cattle starve upon the hills—nay worse,
The foe, swoll'n up to monstrous size, now seems
Hideous and huge as nightmares in our dreams.
Food he no longer finds in fruit or flower,
But, pressed for sustenance, must now devour
Man, man himself !   The caterpillar soon
Will be the last live thing beneath the moon !
To save this anticlimax, if we can,
We have come hither, I and yonder man,

Who tells me—and I know not if he lies—
That at the Pole, beyond the snow and ice,
The souls of birds live on in Paradise.
This Paradise once reached, I mean to beg
Two birds of every species in the egg,
Which, hatched at home with artificial heat,
The old ways of love and pairing shall repeat :
Their beaks sweet pasture in our foes shall find,
And so restore the sceptre to Mankind.
As for this icy vessel that you view,
Drawn by these bears,—that's his invention too.
We now had reached the farthest polar shore,
The line past which no travellers explore :
Of progress northwards I myself despair ;
Then Windbag cries, " Domesticate the bear !"
Bright thought ! With kindness and with cakes of oil
We tamed a hundred—these, with painful toil,
We harnessed to this mount of floating ice,
Then put to sea, well pleased with our device.
Had Neptune's wit been equal to such car,
He had sailed so. You have the tale so far.

WINDBAG.

You there, do you see nothing?

MARESNEST.

No, and yes.
No more than ere you spoke, and nothing less.
But you, who're in our crow's-nest, what do you see?

WINDBAG.

Strange sights, with sounds surpassing simile.

MARESNEST.

What sights?   What sounds?

WINDBAG.

You have a fancy?

MARESNEST.

True.

WINDBAG.

Prepare to whet it.

MARESNEST.

Good.

WINDBAG.

Conceive.

MARESNEST.

I do.

WINDBAG.

Conceive, philosopher, conceive St Paul's,
The dome made all of wind, of wind the walls,
And magnify your thought from base to cope,
As much as ant-eggs in a microscope.
Deem this wind-circle spinning without stop
Ten thousand times more swift than any top.
Throughout the whole circumference, breadth and
    height,
Imagine many a surplice, whirling, white ;
As though, in place of tumbling flakes, were seen
The minor canons, choristers, and Dean.
And, just as when the night-gusts rise and fall,
Suppose there issued from this windy wall
A dreary dirge, which all the world would grant
More doleful far than a Gregorian chant.

MARESNEST.

Pigeons!   I like the thought.

WINDBAG.

This simile
Will show you all things that I hear and see.

MARESNEST.

These are those winds, which, blowing, as they say,
'Twixt the magnetic poles, prevent all way,
And beat the sailor back ; but of the wails
I must protest I know no travellers' tales.

WINDBAG.

Hush ! for we enter now the windy ring,
And you may hear distinctly what they sing.

*(The iceberg is drawn into the Cyclone
of Purgatory, the region of extreme
cold. Innumerable throngs of human
souls are seen driving with the wind.)*

CHORUS OF HUMAN SOULS.

Mortals who attempt the seas
Where man's breath and blood must freeze—
You whom Fortune, by despite,
Destiny, or daring, carry
Farther in the four months' night
Than M'Clintock, Sabine, Parry,
Hayes, or Kane—
Say, we charge ye, why ye come
Where humanity is dumb ;
Is it but to reeve and harry,
Or for gain,
That you break the arctic barriers where the feathered
     spirits reign?

Are you whalers, blown astray
In the chase through Baffin's Bay?
Or men tired of the sun,
Human thought and speech and feature,
That you seek, what all things shun,
Night, that hides each kind and creature?
Have hard times
Driven you up, in hopes of food,
To this landless latitude?

Know ye not, indeed, that Nature
In these climes
For our race produces nothing but requital for our
    crimes ?

Back, we do beseech ye, back
To the ice-floe and the pack !
If your hand has driven a quill,
Clipped a wing, or plucked a feather,
Were your purpose good or ill,
Ye are ruined altogether,
Body and soul !
We were men who speak these words,
But for harm we did the birds
Now are beaten in this weather,
Past control,
Round the Paradise that holds the Aviary of the Pole.

For our crimes are here decreed
Pains proportioned to each deed :
As on earth we played our parts.
Such in Purgatory our measure :
Here, alas ! our human hearts
Are transfigured, and old pleasure

Here is pain :
Some become the birds they slew ;
Others fruitlessly pursue
Feathered phantoms ; all at leisure,
In one strain,
Swear the birds should live for ever could *they* live
  their lives again.

Therefore, back : and if one bird
By your dwelling still be heard
(Since for all this winter none
Pass our barriers), we implore ye
Leave this singer in the sun,
Telling the live world our story :
For 'tis meet
That the infidel should so
By report believe the woe,
Waiting all in Purgatory,
Who entreat
Cruelly with death or dungeon things so simple and so
  sweet.

MARESNEST.

O perdition ! Expedition dark and dolorous ! O
  harsh Fate !

WINDBAG.

Who'd believe such dread *dénoucment* two poor devils
    could await?

MARESNEST.

Devils, ha! 'twas all your deed! you led me here!

WINDBAG.

How could I tell?
I'd an inkling of the Paradise, but never dreamed
    of——

MARESNEST.

Well!
Why do you grow pale and mutter?   One thing, one,
    in this event
Will console me: you will pay for't.

WINDBAG.

I? I've nothing to repent.

MARESNEST.

Nothing!

WINDBAG.

No, I never harmed them in a single feather.

MARESNEST.

What !
How of all those odes you write with—goose-quills ?

WINDBAG.

Mercy ! I forgot !

MARESNEST.

Hapless goose !

WINDBAG.

More hapless poet !

MARESNEST.

And what multiplies the offence
Thousand-fold, you're always scribbling, but you never
mend your pens.

WINDBAG.

Still the goose——

MARESNEST.

Speak not too lightly—you have many a charge to
dread.
Have you ever——

WINDBAG.

No, I never——

MARESNEST.

Slept upon a feather-bed?

WINDBAG.

Out, alas!

MARESNEST.

Or ever relished with a grating of nutmegs
August wheat-ears?

WINDBAG.

Oh!

MARESNEST.

Or partridge *purées-*

WINDBAG.

Ah !—

MARESNEST.

With plovers' eggs ?

WINDBAG.

Guilty, guilty ! All ye birds impeach me ! But why
    mock me, you,
For my innocent ill-doing ?   You have crimes far worse
    to rue !
What dissections !   Egg-collections !   Vast museums
    full of crests !
Crops ! and combs ! and beaks ! and claws ! and
    spurs ! and bushels of birds' nests !
Skeletons ! and embryos !—Monsters that we are !   Is
    this a time
For reproaches ?   Let us rather flee the consequence
    of crime !
Wheel the iceberg southwards !

MARESNEST.

Idiot ! Bring these bears to a full stop !
See their white paws plunging ! Sooner might you bid
    the tempest drop,
Through whose circles we must go to be the prey of
    claw and crop !

But see ! one leaves his comrades and draws near ;
What tumbling strange man-pigeon have we here ?
Ho ! what a somersault !   Unless I err,
This fellow's some Seven-Dials birdcatcher :
His cage, his nets, his call are all arrayed :
He seems to sing some ballad of his trade.

        (*Enter* SOUL OF BIRDCATCHER *tumbling*
           head over heels and singing.)

SOUL OF BIRDCATCHER.

When at close of winter's night
    All the insect world's a-wing ;
When anemones are white ;
    When the first Lent lilies spring ;
When the birds their troths do plight,
    And all feathered lovers sing ;

Eggs of golden plovers reach
In London town a shilling each.

Sweet it is to see the gold
   Brightening on the cowslip tall;
Sweet to hear on lonely wold
   Birds by dawn their lovers call;
Sweet to smell the freshening mould;
   But far sweeter than them all,
Flowers, sweet breath, or songs of lovers,
Are shilling eggs of golden plovers.

Bid them pay, and men will buy
   For their palate magic taste;
Shift the prices, woman's eye
   Leaves the diamond, likes the paste;
If the market run not high,
   Heavenly nectar may go waste;
But each shilling paid discovers
Fresh flavour in the eggs of plovers.

WINDBAG.

What wits are hid 'neath caps of rabbit's fur !
By heaven, this fellow's a philosopher !

The humours of his trade have made him laugh,
And taught him men, like birds, are caught with chaff.
Is not this true?

MARESNEST.

Most true; and I of old
Thought Midas was an ass to starve on gold;
And so, too, thought the gods, and, as appears,
They for this reason gave him asses' ears.
But see, he means to speak : be quiet, pray.

SOUL OF BIRDCATCHER.

Gentlemen, good gentlemen, you are all astray,
You will never find your way.
Follow me, O follow,
I entreat!
You shall see the windy hollow.
Pee-weet! Pee-weet!
Where she makes her hiding-place so cunning, so
    discreet.
'Tis not hard to find,
Only a light scratching in the hollow of the wind,
With olive eggs, all four,
Laid as on the windy moor.

MARESNEST.

What! do the Polar plovers lay wind-eggs?
Quick! follow where he leads us, as he begs.

WINDBAG.

Deep-pondering birds! how well do you devise
A Purgatory to match man's cruelties!
You see he thinks these winds are Salisbury Plain;
We are two rivals come to spoil his gain;
And so he apes the bird whom best he knew,
And would mislead us as the lapwings do.
Hark! "Weet! Pee-weet!" close by, before, behind,
Now in the distance drifting down the wind.

SOUL OF BIRDCATCHER *(heard in the distance)*.

Pee-weet!
Follow, follow!
All the eggs are sweet,
Delicate, and smooth to swallow!
I have looked these twenty years,
Yet not an egg appears.
But if on this windy ground
You a plover's nest have found,

Tell me, I beseech!
Plovers' eggs for London!—eggs a shilling each!

(*Exit* SOUL OF BIRDCATCHER.)

MARESNEST.

Farewell, friend lapwing!   But what smell is this?
O how divine and delicate it is!
How fine and light it floats upon the seas!
Of what does it remind you?

WINDBAG.

Of a breeze
Blown from some range, the mansion-house, to wit,
When twenty thousand larks are on the spit.

MARESNEST.

Well thought! and yet amazement fills my soul
To think what brings a kitchen to the Pole!
A dinner, too!—But we shall know, for look,
Just in the nick of time, here comes the cook.

(*Enter* SOUL OF COOK.)

SOUL OF COOK.

Mais dépêchez-vous, mes messieurs, s'il vous plait,
I have cherché, cherché for you half de day.

Now my leetle preety birds begin to burn ;
Dey are done to—how you call it?—to a turn.
O hélas ! dat I had never left my jack !
Smell you? Ils sont brulés tout! come back, come
    back !

WINDBAG.
MARESNEST. } *At once.*

Hasten, hasten ! What's for dinner?

SOUL OF COOK.

                        Do you veesh
To hear before you taste of de Hundred-Guinea Deesh ?
Has it not been sung by every knife and fork,
" L'extravagance culinaire à l'Alderman " at York ? *
Vy, ven I came here, eighteen Octobers seence,
I dis deesh vas making for your Royal Preence,
Ven half de leeving vorld, cooking all de others,
Swore an oath hereafter to be men and brothers.

* This dish, symbol of philanthropy, was served at York during
the great commemorative banquet after the first Exhibition.   The
history of it is written in a very delicate and appreciative style by
the late M. Soyer in his ' Pantropheon,' a chronicle of the glut-
tonies of various civilisations.   I have preserved the items in the
text.

All de leetle songsters in de voods dat build
Hopped into de keetchen, asking to be killed ;
All who in de open furrows find de seeds,
Or de mountain-berries ; all de farmyard breeds.
Ha ! I see de knife, vile de deesh it shapens
Vith les petits noix of four-and-twenty capons.
Dere vere dindons, fatted poulets, fowls in plenty,
Partridges nine times five, and of pheasants twenty ;
Ten grouse, dat should have had as many covers,
All in dis von deesh vith six preety plovers ;
Forty voodcocks plump and heavy in de scales ;
Pigeons dree good dozens, six-and-dirty quails ;
Ortolans, ma foi ! and a century of snipes ;
But de preetiest of dem all vas twice dree dozen pipes
Of de melodious larks, vich each did clap de ving,
And veeshed de pie vas open, dat dey all might sing.
Ha ! your leeps do smack ! your eyes do seem to shine !
You vill be good appetites ven you vonce do dine !

WINDBAG. ⎫
        ⎬ *At once.*
MARESNEST. ⎭

Hasten, hasten ! tell us where we ought to go.

SOUL OF COOK (*shrugging his shoulders*).

Mais, ma foi ! mes messieurs, but I do not know.
Dere are eighteen autumns scence I left my jack,
And by cap and apron, I have lost de track !
It is near, for always I perceive dis smell ;
And de birds are roasted, dat I know full vell.
Derefore you may tink my soul is on de rack,
Knowing de next second dey vill all be black.
Vell, if come you vill not, you must stay behind.
Adieu ! I go my leetle preety ones to find.

(*Exit* SOUL OF COOK.)

WINDBAG.

Farewell ! and good success.   An artist's soul,
He suffers artist's torments at the Pole !
Fancy ! how hast thou feasted in the frost ?

MARESNEST.

Feeding on nothing, at the stomach's cost.

WINDBAG.

But who comes next ?   Another victim yet ?
Prettiest of girls !   But—O the dear coquette !

C

Was ever drapery so divinely bold?
She's dressed in snow! mere falling flakes enfold
Her form, and veil her from the shoulders down,
Close as the whitest, daintiest dressing-gown.
How crisp appear the neck and wrist-band frill!
I never saw so sweet a deshabille!
Frances of Rimini! I'll hail this dame!—
Most delicate madam, may we know your name?

SOUL OF LADY.

O kind and gracious animal,*
Who in this Purgatory call,
Out of the darkness, on the shade
Of Julia, thrice unhappy maid!
If from a living sunlit coast
You sail, console a banished ghost,
And tell me, in this night of snow,
Of happy Almack's, or the Row!

* "O animal grazíoso e benigno
    Che visitando vai per l'aer perso
    Noi che tignemmo 'l mondo di sanguigno."
                        —DANTE, *Inferno*, c. v. 88.

Say in what carriages what fair
Consume the ice in Berkeley Square;
Or who in shops, with doubtful eye,
Explore the silks they never buy;
And how the hair is dressed in town,
And what the shape of boot and gown.

WINDBAG.

Snow-mantled shadow, would you know
The fashions of the world below,
Still the coiled chignon starward towers;
Still false back-hair falls down in showers;
But now all subtle souls revert
To an abbreviated skirt,
Whose velvet *paniers* just denote
The gown, that else were petticoat.
Nor is such *naïve* attire enough:
Elizabeth's archaic ruff
Rings every neck; besides, they rival,
With a High-Gothic-Hat-Revival,
Old Mother Hubbard, and renew
Arcadianly the buckled shoe,
To show, what's just a trifle shocking,
The dimple of a snowy stocking.

SOUL OF LADY.

Alas, my heart !   No grief so great
As thinking on a happy state
In misery !*   Ah ! dear is power
To female hearts !   O blissful hour,
When Blanche and Flavia joined with me,
Tri-feminine Directory,
Dispensed in latitudes below
The laws of flounce and furbelow,
And held on bird and beast debate,
What lives should die to serve our state !
We changed our statutes with the moon ;
And oft, in January or June,
At deep midnight we would proscribe
Some furry kind or feathered tribe :
At morn we sent the mandate forth ;
Then rose the hunters of the north,
And all the trappers of the west
Bowed at our feminine behest.
Died every seal that dared to rise
To his round air-hole in the ice ;

* " Nessun maggior dolore
Che ricordarsi del tempo felice
Nella miseria."—DANTE, Inferno, c. v. 121.

Died each Siberian fox and hare,
And ermine trapt in snow-built snare.
For us the English fowler set
The ambush of his whirling net ;
And by green Rother's reedy side
The blue kingfisher flashed and died.
His life for us the sea-mew gave
High upon Orkney's lonely wave :
Nor was our queenly power unknown
In Iceland or by Amazon ;
For where the brown duck stripped her breast
For her dear eggs and windy nest,
Three times her bitter spoil was won *
For woman ; and when all was done,
She called her snow-white piteous drake,
Who plucked his bosom for our sake.
No wind that crossed the western main
But wafted tributes of our reign,
Tithes of great tropic forests old,
Humming-birds, all in green and gold,
Which o'er our brows shone dazzling down,
Regalia meet for woman's crown.

* See Hartwig's ' Polar World ' for the manner of taking eider-down.

O bare, O weather-beaten brow !
Once how adorned ! how graceless now !
These flakes that wrap my body, white
As softest eider, burn and bite ;
I wander sleeplessly through snows,
Which once to think of was repose.
But who are ye who in such time,
Blown hither from a temperate clime,
Seek, and alive, the inhuman Pole,
Where the bird-spirits have control ?
Come ye by purpose or astray ?
Far-wandering men, your errand say.

WINDBAG.

Lady, whose worth and woes to hear
Exact the tributary tear,
We come from England and sunshine,
A treaty with the birds to sign.
Seven days we've sailed upon this ice,
And see not yet their Paradise ;
But you, who know these regions, say
How much still waits us of the way.

SOUL OF LADY.

Upon the outskirts of this wind
The temperature will grow more kind ;
Then the Egg-Latitude you greet,
The Limbo of the Obsolete ;
For Man in Purgatory's linked
To Paradise by Birds extinct.

WINDBAG.

A Limbo !   And of Eggs you say ?

SOUL OF LADY.

Yes ; buried far from light of day,
Within the darkness of the shell
Myriads of hapless embryos dwell,
Whom addling Destiny oppressed
In incubation on the nest,
And from their brooding mother snatched,
While the young chicken was unhatched.
Souls too are here whom Time debarred
From Paradise, or Nature marred ;
Some born devoid of wings, and some
Before the days of Christendom,—

Ere Paradise was formed and filled
With happier birds of smaller build—
All now extinct in the ages' course,
The Roc, Dinornis, or Cock-horse.
Now these imperfect souls outside,
Each in his Egg-shell must abide,—
The Egg, first cradle of their race,
So now in death their dwelling-place,
A Limbo dark and mediate,*
Not like sweet Paradise's state,
But happier far than Purgatory,
Reserved for Man.

* Compare Virgil's Limbo of imperfect lives, and Dante's of unbaptised souls :—

> " Continuo auditæ voces, vagitus et ingens,
> Infantumque animæ flentes, *in limine primo:*
> Quos dulcis vitæ exsortes et ab ubere raptos
> Abstulit atra dies, et funere mersit acerbo."
>
> —VIRGIL, *Æneid*, vi. 426.

> " Le turbe, ch 'eran molte e grandi,
> E' d'infanti e di femmine e di viri.
> Lo buon Maestro a me : Tu non dimandi
> Che spiriti son questi che tu vedi ?
> Or vo' che sappi, innanzi che più andi,
> Ch' ei non peccaro : e s' egli hanno mercedi
> Non basta perch' e' non ebber battesmo
> Ch' é porta della Fede che tu credi."
>
> —DANTE, *Inferno*, c. iv. 30.

Prodigious story !

SOUL OF LADY.

Well, you will seek the Porter's gate,
Which is the Roc's Egg designate.
(Greet you the Ancient Chicken well ;
He will admit you through his shell.)
Beyond in the inner circle lies
The Hyperborean Paradise.
Yet stay ! 'Twere better—trust a friend—
Your lives with Esquimaux to spend,
Than seek this Paradise, where all
Are to mankind inimical.
For there, in daring trespass found,
You in some bird's-nest may be bound,
Be tortured by inventive wits,
Playing Prometheus to the tits,
Pinned to the earth by sharp goose-quills,
Impaled upon woodpeckers' bills,
Or whirled through space in tiniest shell
Of wrens ! Be warned, I say ! Farewell !

(*Exit* SOUL OF LADY.)

MARESNEST.

On, on to Limbo ! Did you hear ?
The Roc's Egg ! Perish every fear !
O palæontologic sea !
Was ever traveller blest like me ?
Now is the time and here the station
For a new Theory of Creation !
That for your bones, ye *savants*, skilled
Your fancy-Mammoths hence to build !
(Snapping his fingers.)

Your mummy-fossils wedged between
Oolite beds and Eocene !
My certainty I shall derive
From a Roc-embryo all alive.
Yet when I think, my cheek grows pale ;
What theories tremble in the scale !
Will fate incline to Noah's ark,
Myself, Hugh Miller, or Lamarck ?
Be brass, my bosom ! bear each shock !
And now for Limbo and the Roc !

(*They arrive in sight of shore. The Limbo, a circle formed of many eggs, of enormous size and different colours, runs like a wall round the extreme edge.*)

WINDBAG.

See, see, the land!   The great Egg-Mountain, lo!
Just as old Sinbad viewed it long ago.*
All round it lie vast eggs of various hue,
Of Moa and Dinornis, green, white, blue.
So shone, methinks, those dazzling rings that ran
Round the bright battlements of Agbatan,
Whereof Herodotus so sweetly writes.†

MARESNEST.

Or Easter eggs of the pre-Adamites.
But see! we are arrived.   Go, call this thing!
And loudly on his egg-shell knock and ring.

---

* "I made a mark at the place where I stood, and went round the egg, measuring its circumference: and lo! it was fifty full paces; and I meditated upon some means of gaining an entrance into it."—Second Voyage of Sinbad of the Sea.

† Herodotus, describing the seven coloured walls of Ecbatana, says: "The battlements of the first circle are white; of the second, black; of the third, purple; of the fourth, blue; of the fifth, scarlet.   These battlements are all painted of those colours: the two last have coats respectively of silver and gold."—Herodotus, i. 98.

THE PARADISE OF BIRDS.

WINDBAG (*knocking*).

Ho! porter! Rat-tat-tat! Undo your door!
Sweet chicken! You within! I say, once more
Rat-tat-tat-tat! Be quick! Lift up your latch!
Keep us not shivering: 'tis full time to hatch!

MARESNEST.

He is perhaps grown addled in the cold.

WINDBAG.

You embryo! you chick! Be not too bold!
I will devise a saucepan on the sea,
And hard-hard-boil you to infinity;
Or break your shell, as once indeed before
Sinbad's companions served your ancestor.

ROC (*from within his shell*).

Who are you?

MARESNEST.

Bipeds bound for Paradise.

ROC.

Whence flew you here?

MARESNEST.

We came upon the ice.

ROC.

Upon the ice !   But have you wings, my chicks?

MARESNEST.

No; we're great-grandsons of the Apteryx.

ROC.

But you have beaks and talons, I daresay?

MARESNEST.

Yes—with variety.

ROC.

And feathers, eh?

MARESNEST.

No; for our first forefathers moulted all.

ROC.

What is your family?

MARESNEST.

Genus Animal.

ROC.

Are you extinct?

MARESNEST.

Not yet.   Nor shall we die,
I hope, but soon increase and multiply.

ROC.

But what's your claim to enter Limbo, then?

MARESNEST.

Our sovereign rank in Nature : we are Men.

ROC.

Kluck ! why, you then have blood within your veins
" Of that small infantry warred on by cranes."

And yet perhaps your lineage you can trace
From some primeval half-extinguished race,
In breeding scarce below the birds of air,
Maori, Sioux, Tasmanian, Delaware?

MARESNEST.

Inhabitant of Limbo, know our birth
Is Anglo-Saxon; we are lords of earth.
In every other zone we dispossess,
Or make the aborigines progress;
Which means we give to every naked nation
The choice of broadcloth or extermination.
Now impulse to Perfection bids us rise
Northwards, to win the Pole and Paradise;
Therefore no longer keep us in the cold;
We spare no useless thing because 'tis old.
Not now with Eastern Sinbad are you matched:
Once more I say,—Admit us and BE HATCHED !

ROC.

O children of Extinction ! Souls that sleep
Within the heart of your ancestral keep!
Hear what blaspheming threats these strangers roll
On us, and in the precincts of the Pole !

What welcome shall we give, what answer, say,
To these weak wingless things of yesterday?

CHORUS OF EXTINCT EMBRYOS (*in the shell*).

What newfangled impious words
Have shaken our eggs, O ye Birds?
Have rung an alarm on the shell
To our souls in the innermost cell?
What is this that is uttered?
Inform us, we beg,
Ye, whose fathers have fluttered
Or slept on one leg!
Shall we boil? or be buttered?
Will they fry, or, alack!
Pound, crunch us, or crack?
Or whatever the verb
That can chiefly disturb,
By saucepan or boiler,
With pepper and oil, or
With salt and nutmeg,
In a dire Revolution,
Our great Constitution,
Our ancient, divine, unimprovable Egg.

Out of chaos in ages of gold
Our fathers invented a mould,
That our race to its uttermost day
Might for ever be hatched in this way.
Then, ye egg-loving Tories,
Though, shut in the cell,
We birds bid our glories
Eternal farewell,
Though we know but in stories
Of lives that could sing,
Fold and flutter the wing,
While we in poor plight,
Mere yellow and white,
Despite all endeavour,
Shall chickens be—never ;
Yet strong is the spell,
That bids our alliance
Crow back its defiance
To the fools who would cobble and tinker our Shell.

Who is he who aspires to improve
Incubation, and alter its groove ?
Some great philosophical bird,

Who has thought, or in travel has heard,
Of a fresh, altogether
Fantastical, plan—
A phœnix in feather,
A king in our clan,
Who, amid wind and weather,
Has grown to old age
A most radical sage?
No—a thing of two legs,
Yet not born out of eggs,
Nor ancient, but rather
Scarce knows his grandfather,
Who lives but a span,
Too broad in the haunches
For nesting in branches,
Roturier, roundhead, ridiculous Man.

This Man, among creatures of earth
The latest, most impotent birth,
Is of animals far the most bold
Against all things established and old.
His envy runs riot
In cottage and grange ;

Abroad he seeks quiet,
At home he would range ;
Entertainment and diet,
Trade, treasure, peace, strife,
Friends, children, and wife,
His land and his laws,
He will leave without cause,
Beholding through Fancy
A bright necromancy
In all that is strange,
Who, finding each second
His hopes were misreckoned,
Despairing of Happiness, bargains for Change.

But is novelty drained to the dregs
That he comes to our obsolete Eggs,
Our great institutions to storm,
And demolish our shells by Reform?
What are sixty-year sages
To Egg-shells sublime,
That have hatched through all stages
The chicks of each clime ;
That are old as the ages,

THE PARADISE OF BIRDS.

And fixed as the stars;
That, through jostles and jars,
Have endured in despite,
With the yolk and the white,
With the big end and little,
Not changing a tittle,
While birds in the lime,
Spite of fire, wind, and waters,
Have laid sons and daughters,
Secure from the elements, scornful of Time?

Shall we see this degenerate foe
In the home of our forefathers?   No!
Ho! ye embryos of beaks and of claws,
Let us strike for our customs and laws!
Let us muster and rally,
Be firm and stand fast!
No more shilly-shally;
This line is our last!
Yet make no rash sally,
But watch at each end,
The weak points to defend,
And at every crack
Let us cackle and clack

To affright with our babel
This biped unstable,
This Oonoclast
Who with all Tweedledeedom
Assaults chicken Freedom,
Palladium of Limbo, the Egg of the Past.

ROC.

Well crowed, sweet chickens! Impious bipeds, hear!
Tempt not our vengeance, but our eggs revere!

MARESNEST.

Advance! Blow up the trumpets! sound bassoons!
On with the battery of ten thousand spoons!
Advance the salt-cellars! the rollers heave!
On, on! This bragging is all make-believe.
An addled brain Dutch courage oft imparts:
Behind yon shells there are but chicken-hearts.

ROC.

How would you tremble could you see my beak!

MARESNEST.

Perhaps. But, till I see it, faith is weak.

ROC.

Some of your ancestors obtained a sight
Of my forefathers, and report their might.

MARESNEST.

What naturalist?

ROC.

Why, Sinbad of the sea.

MARESNEST.

He never studied Natural History.

ROC.

In Madagascar Marco Polo heard *—

---

* " The people of this island report, that at a certain season
of the year an extraordinary kind of bird, which they call a roc,
makes its appearance from the southern region. In form it is said
to resemble an eagle, but it is incomparably larger, being so large
and strong as to seize an elephant with its talons, and to lift it into
the air, whence it lets it fall to the ground, in order that when
dead it may prey upon the carcase." The grand Khan, says
Marco Polo, sent to inquire about this bird. "When the mes-
sengers returned to the presence of his majesty, they brought with
them (as I have heard) a feather of a roc, positively affirmed to
have measured ninety spans, and the quill part to have been two

MARESNEST.

Munchausen tales at second-hand or third.
But *savants* have not mentioned you, not one—
Linnæus, Humboldt, Cuvier, Audubon.

ROC.

No ; for I was extinct before their days.

MARESNEST.

Extinct !   You show your weakness in your phrase :
And, by presumption, a plain proof you give
That your forefathers had no strength to live.

ROC.

How think you, then, our race grew obsolete ?

MARESNEST.

First, I suppose, you'd not enough to eat.

ROC.

Bah ! when our parents, as the truth affirms,
Fed the young bird with elephants for worms.

palms in circumference. This surprising exhibition afforded his
majesty extreme pleasure, and upon those by whom it was pre-
sented he bestowed valuable gifts."—Marco Polo's Travels (Mars-
den's translation), c. 36.

MARESNEST.

Or of your ancestors one chanced to trip,
And some disease contracted, say the pip,
Which, breeding in his heirs, impaired at length
Their constitutions, and sapped up their strength.

ROC.

Pooh ! pooh !

MARESNEST.

Or, it your blood escaped disease,
Perhaps your parasites *—

ROC.

You mean my—

MARESNEST.

Please !

Just see the delicacy of the Greek !
Or else—

* "A highly capable judge, Dr Falconer, believes that it is
chiefly insects which, from incessantly harassing and weakening
the elephant in India, check its increase ; and this was Bruce's
conclusion with respect to the African elephant in Abyssinia."—
Darwin's ' Origin of Species.'

ROC.

In short, you think that, growing weak,
And, pressed by strong competitors, our brood
Could not sustain the unequal strife for food.

MARESNEST.

Precisely : if 'twere not some cause like this,
What would become of my hypothesis?

ROC.

Hear, then, the truth ; and, honouring blood and
    birth,
Respect the oldest family on earth.
Born in volcanic times, the Roc's first sire
Bequeathed them giant stature, souls of fire,
But lives so long as forced them to behold
The birds grow dwarfish as the world grew cold.
In these succeeding ages, silent wits,
They were *ennuyé* with the chattering Tits ;
And dwelt apart in unfrequented nooks,
Scorning the loud Republic of the Rooks.
Yet, in degree to destiny resigned,
Though mourning much o'er their degenerate kind,

Life was not yet intolerable, till Man
All creatures in the downhill race outran.
No place so lonely where they hatched their young,
But there he brought his merchandise and tongue.*
Then the Roc remnant, one by one, withdrew,
Till of the ancient race remained but two ;
Whereof the hen, when she had lost her mate,
Flew here, and laid this egg at Limbo Gate,
Folded maternal wings on either side,
And so, in act of incubation, died.

MARESNEST.

Ah, bah !   Inventions of your cleric cocks ! '
You speak like birds unhatched and orthodox.
Why, all geology's a flat denial ;
You'd have more light, could you have thumbed a
     Lyell.
That for your family ! (*snapping his fingers.*)   Now I
     could swear
You think you spring of one primeval pair,
With claws and feathers all at once supplied
By Providence, to please patrician pride ?

---

* For instance, Sinbad's Valley of Diamonds.

ROC.

Perhaps.

MARESNEST.

From whence d'you get your beak and wing ?

ROC.

You said—from Providence.

MARESNEST.

There's no such thing.*

ROC.

Eh ! What ! You're poking fun.   By whose direction
Was this Egg made ?

MARESNEST.

By Natural Selection.

ROC.

What's that ?

---

* "See," says old Strepsiades, in 'The Clouds,' "what a fine
thing education is ! My Pheidippides, there is no Zeus."   "Well,
who is there then ?" asks his son.   " Whirl is king," answers the
father, " having turned out Zeus."—Aristophanes, Nubes, 826.

MARESNEST.

    The rise of Species : can it be
You know not how it was? Then hear from me.
Ho ! ye obsolete wings in the outset of things,
 Which the clergy Creation miscall,
There was nought to perplex by shape, species, or sex ;
 Indeed, there was nothing at all,
But a motion most comic of dust-motes atomic,
 A chaos of decimal fractions,
Of which each under Fate was impelled to his mate
 By Love or the law of Attractions.
So jarred the old world, in blind particles hurled,
 And Love was the first to attune it,
Yet not by prevision, but simple collision—
 And this was the cause of the Unit.
That such was the feat, which evolved light and heat,
 A thousand analogies hint ;
For instance, the spark from the hoof in the dark,
 Or the striking of tinder and flint.
Of the worlds thus begun the first was the Sun,
 Who, wishing to round off his girth,
Began to perspire with great circles of fire--
 And this was the cause of the Earth.
Soon desiring to pair, Fire, Water, Earth, Air,

To monogamous custom unused,
All joined by collusion in fortunate fusion,
  And so the Sponge-puzzle produced.
Now the Sponge had of yore many attributes more
  Than the power to imbibe or expunge,
And his leisure beguiled with the hope of a child.

CHORUS.

O philoprogenitive Sponge !

MARESNEST.

Then Him let us call the first Parent of all,
  Though the clergy desire to hoodwink us ;
For He gave to the Earth the first animal birth,
  And conceived the Ornithorhyncus.

CHORUS.

Conceived the Ornithorhyncus !

MARESNEST.

Yes : who, as you have heard, has a bill like a bird,
  But hair and four legs like a beast,
And possessed in his kind a more provident mind
  Than you'd e'er have presumed from the priest :

For he saw in the distance the strife for existence,
  That must his grandchildren betide,
And resolved, as he could, for their ultimate good,
  A remedy sure to provide.
With that, to prepare each descendant and heir
  For a different diet and clime,
He laid, as a test, four eggs in his nest—
  But he only laid two at a time.
On the first he sat still, and kept using his bill,
  That the head in his chicks might prevail.
Ere he hatched the next young, head downwards he
    slung
  From the branches, to lengthen his tail.
Conceive how he watched till his chickens were hatched,
  With what joy he observed that each brood
Were unlike at the start, had their dwellings apart,
  And distinct adaptations for food.
Thereafter each section by Nature's selection
  Proceeded to husband and wive,
And the truth can't be blinked that the weak grew ex-
    tinct,
  While the lusty continued to thrive.
Eggs were laid as before, but each time more and more
  Varieties struggled and bred,

Till one end of the scale dropped its ancestor's tail,
    And the other got rid of his head.
From the bill, in brief words, were developed the birds,
    Unless our tame pigeons and ducks lie ;
From the tail and hind legs, in the second-laid eggs,
    The Apes and—Professor Huxley.

CHORUS.

The Apes, and Professor Huxley !

MARESNEST.

Yes ; one Protoplasm, connecting the chasm
    'Twixt Mammal, and Reptile, and Roc,
With millions of dozens of fungus first cousins,
    Reduces the world to one stock ;
And though Man has a place from the Sponge at the
    base
    In variety farthest removed,
And has managed to reach what he calls soul and
    speech,
    Yet his blood is by language approved.
For instance, the tribe that contrives to imbibe,
    While the friends, who believe in them, plunge

Their hands with mad pranks into Railways and Banks,
   We term the variety Sponge.
And perhaps like our Sire, as all classes mount higher,
   We shall merge into Oneness again,
Our species absorb all the rest in its orb,
   And Birds, Beasts, and Fishes be Men.

CHORUS.

What! Birds, Beasts, and Fishes be Men!

ROC.

O harder to brook than republican rook!
   More prating than pies every one!
Do you dare thus to scoff, and by Limbo? Be off!
                   (*Puts his head out of his shell.*)

MARESNEST.

O pigeons!

WINDBAG.

Holloa! Do you run?
Now Greek will meet Greek.

MARESNEST.

O ye stars, what a beak !

WINDBAG.

You surely won't let him escape,
But will analyse well the contents of his shell.

MARESNEST.

How yellow and grim was his gape !

WINDBAG.

Do you order a halt ?

MARESNEST.

Why indeed to assault
Such a fortress—

WINDBAG.

Just now you were hearty
As gentle John Bright, or as Mill, the polite,
When he scolded the great "stupid party."

MARESNEST.

We must think of some trick to outwit this fierce chick.

E

WINDBAG.

I've ever observed that in pleading,
All your Radical sect has one vital defect :
  You can't see the worth of good breeding.
Had you coaxed this old bird with some honey-sweet
    word,
  He had welcomed us both ; but you dish up
Hot sauce, and at once set him down as a dunce,
  As when you are baiting a bishop.
You have managed to lay all his plumes the wrong way :
  I must stroke them to rights with my rhymes ;
And, your folly to hedge, shall your teeth set on edge,
  While I glorify——

MARESNEST.

What ?

WINDBAG.

Good old Times.

MARESNEST.

You !

WINDBAG.

Without more demur, ho ! obsolete sir,
Let your head to your servant be showed.

Me the Muses inspire, and my heart is on fire,
  Your Limbo to praise in an ode.

                    (Roc *puts out his head.*)

O unhatched Bird, so high preferred,
    As porter of the Pole,
Of beakless things, who have no wings,
    Exact no heavy toll.
If this my song its theme should wrong,
    The theme itself is sweet ;
Let others rhyme the unborn time,
    I sing the Obsolete.

And first, I praise the nobler traits
    Of birds preceding Noah,
The giant clan, whose meat was Man,
    Dinornis, Apteryx, Moa.
These, by the hints we get from prints
    Of feathers and of feet,
Excelled in wits the later tits,
    And so are obsolete.

I sing each race whom we displace
    In their primeval woods,

While Gospel Aid inspires Free-Trade
    To traffic with their goods.
With Norman Dukes the still Sioux
    In breeding might compete ;
But where men talk the tomahawk
    Will soon grow obsolete.

I celebrate each perished State ;
    Great cities ploughed to loam ;
Chaldæan kings ; the Bulls with wings ;
    Dead Greece ; and dying Rome.
The Druids' shrine may shelter swine,
    Or stack the farmer's peat ;
'Tis thus mean moths treat finest cloths,
    Mean men the obsolete.

Shall nought be said of theories dead ?
    The Ptolemaic system ?
Figure and phrase, that bent all ways
    Duns Scotus liked to twist 'em ?
Averrhoes' thought ? and what was taught
    In Salamanca's seat ?
Sihons and Ogs ? and showers of frogs ?
    Sea-serpents obsolete ?

Pillion and pack have left their track ;
  Dead is "the Tally-ho."
Steam rails cut down each festive crown
  Of the old world and slow.
Jack-in-the-Green no more is seen,
  Nor Maypole in the street ;
No mummers play on Christmas-day ;
  St George is obsolete.

O Fancy, why hast thou let die
  So many a frolic fashion ?
Doublet and hose, and powdered beaux ?
  Where are thy songs, whose passion
Turned thought to fire in knight and squire,
  While hearts of ladies beat ?
Where thy sweet style, ours, ours erewhile ?
  All this is obsolete.

In Auvergne low potatoes grow
  Upon volcanoes old ;
The moon, they say, had her young day,
  Though now her heart is cold ;
Even so our earth, sorrow and mirth,
  Seasons of snow and heat,

Checked by her tides in silence glides
To become obsolete.

The astrolabe of every babe
Reads in its fatal sky,
" Man's largest room is the low tomb—
Ye all are born to die."
Therefore this theme, O Birds, I deem
The noblest we may treat ;
The final cause of Nature's laws
Is to grow obsolete.

ROC.

By all the Dodos ! these are thoughts of weight,
Most venerable, wise, and out of date ;
A little off the mark : methinks, your words
Should have said less of men and more of birds.
But that you love the great Extinct is clear ;
The burden, too, 's most pleasing to my ear.
Little I thought, while I possessed this cell,
Souls without beaks should pass through Limbo's
        shell ;
But now your words my heart completely win ;
I can refuse you nothing ; pray come in.

(MARESNEST *and* WINDBAG *pass through
the Roc's Egg into the Earthly Paradise, an enchanted region of twilight
and gentle temperature, abounding in
trees, grass hollows, and fresh water.*)

WINDBAG.

O magic clime! O mild and temperate air!

MARESNEST.

Thrice happy birds! how ill with these compare
All homes of yours I've found in realms of Man.
In Paraguay, the Feroes, or Japan!
See, here are burrows for the puffins' homes,
Grey lichens whence the titmice build their domes,
Broad hawthorn for the chaffinches, and high
Spruce for the rook, the ringdove, and the pic.
Here too are streams, where on the outreaching
    boughs
The water-hen may hang her balanced house.
And each sub-polar dainty, down or seed,
Springs here by magic. Paradise indeed!

WINDBAG.

Either I'm tranced in some delightful spell,
Or well-known voices cleave the darkened dell.
That was the starling's whistle ; and all hail !
" Jug, jug !"   It is, it is the nightingale !
Now I distinguish more, the blackbird mark,
Redstart, ring-ousel, redpole, linnet, lark,
Full-throated blackcap, and sedge-warbler meek :
There came a "cuckoo !" there a pipit's " peek!"
O sounds the sweeter since so long unheard !
Thus once in merry England sang each bird.
Ha ! now I think, it is St Valentine :
Sit down, and hear a thousand bills combine.

LARK (*heard singing in the dark.*)

Awake! awake ! 'tis the early gloaming !
    The night is parted ! the stars are pale !
O ye souls on your roosts, the sun is coming ! *
    Awake, light-hearted ; his advent hail !
He will change sweet sleep into waking brightness ;
    He will spread warm weathers about the Pole ;

---

* The sun in the Arctic regions reappears on February 17.

He comes to cherish our hearts with lightness,
With warmth our feathers, with song the soul.

Awake! awake! leave your winter slumber!
Our saint, ye lovers, leads up the Spring;
St Valentine listens for notes in number;
Then quit your covers, ye birds, and sing!
Let us sing, as we sang in our old world's leisure,
In each oak-portal, on English knolls,
A song of Paradise, endless pleasure,
The life immortal, the rest of souls!

(*Semi-chorus of* THRUSHES, LINNETS, *and*
BLACKCAPS.)

Hark! hark!
A voice has come,
Through the leaves in the dark,
Clear and ringing,
Bidding our souls to be no more dumb,
But be up and singing!
It is the lark;
He has seen the rays of the rising sun
From the Ocean springing:

And he bids us arise,
And give thanks, each one,
For the Polar skies, and for Paradise,
And the long delights that the day is bringing.

O windless haven of delight !
O equal bliss of day and night !
O rest of birds ! what songs suffice
To exalt thy glories, Paradise?
Here in clear streams all day we dip
Our beaks, yet suffer from no pip.
No longer over-cold or wet
Do we feel heart-ache, care, or fret.
Our throat and eye are ever clear ;
Nor do we moult for all the year.

Here neither drought nor deluge breeds
Harsh competition for the seeds ;
Nor, as on earth in winters rough,
Do insects fail : all find enough.
Ripe berries here abound, to feast
All souls, the greatest and the least :
The ruddy fruit unguarded drops ;

And here for the grain-loving crops
Are seeds of every size and shape,
The oily hemp and the sweet rape ;
And, for the slender bills and small,
Fresh flies and gnats ambrosial.

Here in the moonlight prowls no stoat.
The burglar of the sleeping cote.
The very birds, which seemed on earth
Bandits and cannibals by birth,
Dwell here in brotherhood, alike
The owl, the sparrow-hawk, the shrike.
The pies, once gluttons, no more strive
Upon their neighbours' eggs to thrive ;
And even the cuckoo has confessed,
And, honest housewife, builds a nest.

Four months in roost and darkness run :
Four months we feel perpetual sun ;
Ere he be risen, in dale and grove,
We through the twilight sing of Love :
And while he slowly downward goes,
We hymn the pleasures of Repose.

So dwells each soul that sings or flies
In our terrestrial Paradise.

Semi-chorus of SWALLOWS.

Unbounded joys ye sing, and yet
One peerless privilege forget.
Of all the thousand earthly pests
That stole our down, despoiled our nests,
And took our lives, ye may aver
The worst was Man the birdcatcher.
For know, O birds, that in old time,
When swallows flew from clime to clime,
In torrid sun or temperate air,
This Man was with us everywhere.
Oft in Egyptian pilgrimage
We met him with his nets and cage :
And when in April we flew forth
To take the summer to the north,
He whistled there on sunny wall,
An urchin with his clapper call.
There too his last year's scarecrow stood,
Rain-drenched and rotten by the wood ;
His scarlet rags above the grain
Fluttered the larks on Salisbury Plain ;

THE PARADISE OF BIRDS.

And later on green garden-plots,
Under the wall of apricots,
His rusty, single-barrelled gun
Brought down the blackbird in the sun.

This land, this happy land alone,
He may not reach ; it is our own.
For if he pass the icy pack,
The winds of Heaven will blow him back ;
And lack of food his heart constrains,
And bitter frost congeals his veins.

In Paradise, remote from fear,
Our souls abide in endless cheer ;
But Man our enemy must still
Brood on in his sub-polar ill,
Heart-aching, feverish, poor, and chill.

Thou, Nightingale, who at thy choice
Biddest us sorrow or rejoice,
And sittest in deep leaves apart,
Fathoming thine own lonely heart,

Sing to us now of Man ; relate
His birth, his miserable state.
Thy sweetness, solacing the ear,
Will make privation sound more drear ;
And in his bitterness each breast
Will seem incomparably blest.

NIGHTINGALE.

Man that is born of a woman,
    Man, her un-web-footed drake,
Featherless, beakless, and human,
    Is what he is by mistake.
For they say that a sleep fell on Nature
    In midst of the making of things ;
And she left him a two-legged creature,
    But wanting in wings.

CHORUS.

Kluk-uk-uk ! kio ! coo !
Peeweet ! caw, caw ! cuckoo !
Tio ! tuwheet ! tuwhoo ! pipitopan !
Chilly, unfeathered, wingless, short-tethered,
Restless, bird-nestless, unfortunate Man !

NIGHTINGALE.

Therefore, ye birds, in all ages,
    Man, in his hopes of the sky,
Caught us, and clapped us in cages,
    Seeking instruction to fly.
But neither can cloister nor college
    Accord to the scholar this boon,
Nor centuries give him the knowledge
    We get in a moon.

CHORUS.

Kluk-uk-uk ! &c.
Moon-and-star-hoping, doomed to low groping,
Fretting, bird-netting, tyrannical Man !

NIGHTINGALE.

Thoughts he sends to each planet,
    Uranus, Venus, and Mars,
Soars to the centre to span it,
    Numbers the infinite stars.
But he never will mount as the swallows,
    Who dashed round his steeples to pair,
Or hawked the bright flies in the hollows
    Of delicate air.

CHORUS.

Kluk-uk-uk ! &c.
Gross, astronomical, star-gazing, comical,
Hazy, moon-crazy, fantastical Man !

NIGHTINGALE.

Custom he does not cherish :
 Eld makes room for the young ;
Kingdoms prosper and perish ;
 Tongue gives place unto tongue.
But we live by the laws that were shown us;
 In England the song in my beak
Was the same that my sire at Colonus
 Had sung to the Greek.

CHORUS.

Kluk-uk-uk ! &c.
Mushroom in dating, ancestor-hating,
Smattering, much-chattering, competitive Man !

NIGHTINGALE.

Gold he pursues like a shadow ;
 Then, as he grasps at his goal,
Far, afar off, El-Dorado
 Shines like a star on his soul.

THE PARADISE OF BIRDS.

So his high expectation brings sorrow,
  And plenty increases his needs ;
But the birds took no thought for the morrow,
  Secure of their seeds.

CHORUS.

Kluk-uk-uk ! &c.
Man the great sailor, petty retailer,
Wealthy, unhealthy, luxurious Man !

NIGHTINGALE.

Therefore his heart, unforgiving,
  Grudged us the down on our coats,
Envied the ease of our living,
  Hated the tune in our notes ;
And he snared us, too careless and merry,
  Or compassed our death with his gun,
As we wheeled round the currant and cherry,
  Or bathed in the sun.

CHORUS.

Kluk-uk-uk ! &c.
Close-fisted warden, pest of the garden,
Hooting, thrush-shooting, malevolent Man !

NIGHTINGALE.

Little, so low was his spirit,
    Deemed he the bird had a soul;
Thought that we went to inherit
    Endless repose at the Pole:
For his soul has no powers of expansion,
    And fears, if she see not, to trust;
So she makes of her money a mansion—
    She cleaves to the dust.

CHORUS.

Kluk-uk-uk! &c.
Golden-calf-maker, money-moon-raker,
Blinded, mole-minded, material Man!

NIGHTINGALE.

Though not a sigh float hither,
    Crossing the circle of snows,
Deem not below us fair weather
    Gladdens mankind with repose.
Still the wages of earth he is winning,
    Lamentation, and labour, and pain;
As it was in the very beginning,
    And so shall remain.

CHORUS.

Kluk-uk-uk ! &c.
Monarch of reason, slave of each season,
Wizened, imprisoned, ex-Paradised Man !

MARESNEST (*starting up*).

O pigeons ! I can bear no more !
I shall——

WINDBAG.

Be quiet, I implore !

MARESNEST.

What ! should a naturalist endure
Such insults calmly ?

WINDBAG.

To be sure ;
Think where you are.   (*Seizing him.*)

MARESNEST.

Hands off, I say ;
I must be at them !

WINDBAG.

Gently, pray !
You'll have them on us, claw and beak.

MARESNEST.

Away ! I care not ! I will speak !
You nightingale ! you ass ! you lie !
You daw ! you pessimist ! you pie !
You *dilettante* croaking frog !
You paid court-poet of King Log !
By Heaven ! I think you are the soul
Of Lord George Bentinck !   O you mole !
What nonsense have you dared to say
To me ! and at this time of day !
Thoughts quite pre-Adamite, the views
Of Pio Nono's Jesuit crews !
Ah ! could I come at you, I'd stop
Your singing !   I'd choke out your crop !

CHORUS.

Kluk-uk-uk ! kio ! coo !
Peeweet ! caw, caw ! cuckoo !
Tio ! tuwheet ! tuwhoo ! ck-ck-ckys !
Quack, quack ! hoo-pooh-pooh-pooh !

Be-be-off! shoo shoo!
Hoo-hoo-dedoo-saru?   Ek-ek-ek!
I-s-s-s!

WINDBAG.

Ye Muses! what a hiss was there!
Like calico it rent the air!
The voice of twenty thousand geese,
Defiant, not preluding peace!
All round earth, air, hill, dale, branch, brier,
Crackle and burn with beaks of fire!
The attack advances!   'Tis no sham!
Run, run!

MARESNEST.

Adieu!

WINDBAG.

Be off!

MARESNEST.

I am!

(*They run into different hollow trees.*)

CHORUS.

On, gallant sirs !
With buckling of spurs !
With tossing of crests !
Come from your nests,
Redstart and shrike,
With bills prompt to strike !
Brown sanderlings,
Advance your left wings !
Cranes to the right about !
Wheel in swift flight about !
Scour all the ground !
Every outlet surround !
For a thief by surprise
Despoils Paradise—
Man, the talkative Ape—
And he shall not escape !
Ha, ha !   Do I see
Low-crouched in yon tree ?
It is he ! it is he !
You robber ! you cat !
Take that, that, that, that !

(CHORUS *discover and peck* MARESNEST.)

(*Enter* BIRD OF PARADISE.)

BIRD OF PARADISE.

O chattering souls, whose tongues, too early loosed,
Break throughout Paradise our happy roost !
It is not dawn, yet you have waked your King ;
And as for me, you know I never sing.
I had just dreamed that in Peruvian plants,
At breakfast-time, I found a nest of ants :
Such joy I had not had for many a week ;
And here and there I dashed my active beak ;
And seven I had despatched at the last stroke,
When all at once you chattered, and I woke.
Come now, inform me why, before 'tis light,
You have disturbed the pleasures of my night.

CHORUS.

O best of monarchs ! though 'tis near daybreak,
We would have still kept silence for your sake :
But while we slept, our enemies, we fear,
Have entered Paradise, and one is—here.

BIRD OF PARADISE.

O ants and beetles ! make the wretch come forth !

WINDBAG.

Now must the inventive poet show his worth.

(*Aside.*)

O prince of plumage ! rainbow-feathered soul !

(*Advancing.*)

Lord of long beaks ! high monarch of the Pole !
O hundred-coloured, heaven-descended Bird !
Be just, since great ; condemn us not unheard !

BIRD OF PARADISE.

Another !   Ha ! how many more are you ?

WINDBAG.

O Paragon of plumes, we are but two.

BIRD OF PARADISE.

You have no feathers, nor a soul·appear.

WINDBAG.

Alive and featherless, we venture here.

BIRD OF PARADISE.

Why, then, 'tis clear you've picked our Limbo's lock.

WINDBAG.

No; your great porter let us in, the Roc.

BIRD OF PARADISE.

I see you are a Man.   You have two legs,
But neither beak nor wings.   What want you?

WINDBAG.

Eggs.

BIRD OF PARADISE.

O you that utter thrice unhallowed words!
How have you wronged the Paradise of Birds!
Dare you thus openly infringe our laws?
Is malice, or sheer ignorance, the cause?
If ignorance, you should the laws have known.

WINDBAG.

Nay, we've enough to do to know our own,
Being Englishmen ; but what d'you mean?

BIRD OF PARADISE.

Jackdaw,
Clerk of all Paradise, recite the law.

JACKDAW.

" Whatever soul of herein-namèd things,
Mammals, beasts, quadrupeds, devoid of wings,
Claws, crops, combs, spurs, crests, feathers, bills with
     notes,
To wit, rats, cats, mice, foxes, badgers, stoats,
Weasels, or others, enter, or come nigh,
Near, through, to, into, Paradise—shall die."

MARESNEST (*coming out of his tree*).

Die !   How's that possible, if he's a soul ?

WINDBAG.

How?   Why, by paradox !   (*Aside.*)   You ass !   you
     mole !

BIRD OF PARADISE (*to* JACKDAW).
Proceed.

JACKDAW.

" Whatever biped (save the shape
Hereinbefore declared), to wit, the Ape,
Baboon, Gorilla, Chimpanzee, or Man,
Seek the said place, on the aforesaid plan,

In quest of aught soever, gall or crests,
Of feathers or of down, of eggs or nests,
The soul of the said biped shall be pecked,
Clawed, racked, torn, tattered, as the laws direct."

MARESNEST.

By all the pigeons ! but these laws were made
By some most flat blasphemer of Free-Trade!
The Birds, it seems, have still a predilection
For Spartan closeness and Chinese Protection.
Why, if mankind had framed their statutes so,
What right could Spain have had to Mexico?
Where now were heard our Saxon tongue? and—
    yes !
Where our philosophers? our penny press?
Where had been Cobden ? where Sir Robert Peel?
    and
Where that fair queen of colonies, New Zealand?
O you blind Birds! The strong must win the prize.
Be it Van Diemen's Land or Paradise !

BIRD OF PARADISE.

O profane heart ! O thrice accursèd tongue !

WINDBAG.

Accursèd !   Ah ! if 'twere but glazed and hung !

(Aside.)

Most glorious sir, think not we would presume,
Our crime once proved, to deprecate our doom :
But of our guilt we first would make denial,
And so demand of you a form of trial.

BIRD OF PARADISE.

Why, you were caught red-handed in the act.

WINDBAG.

But justice still is formal and exact.
Besides, we mean to plead in our defence
Mankind's deserts, our inexperience ;
And if this fail, who knows but we may slip
Through the indictment on some legal quip ?

BIRD OF PARADISE.

Now by my beak ! I thank you for these words,
Praising the Habeas Corpus of the Birds.
Ho ! crier, call a jury in the air,
Rook, cuckoo, lapwing, redstart, blackcap, stare,

Owl, bullfinch, seagull, wagtail, falcon, wren ;
Swear all these birds fairly to judge of men ;
Sparrows, surround the prisoners at the bar !
Are all here present whom I've called ?

JURY.

We are.

JACKDAW.

O ye Birds ! will you swear
By the sun, by the air,
By St Valentine's Day,
By April and May,
By beak, claw, and crest,
By the loves of the nest,
And by all incubation,
To judge of this pair
As the laws of our nation
Direct you ?

JURY.

We swear.

(*The* JURY *arrange themselves upon the
bough of a neighbouring tree.*)

CHORUS.

We wish to declare how the Birds of the air
  All high Institutions designed,
And holding in awe, art, science, and law,
  Delivered the same to mankind.
To begin with : of old Man went naked and cold
  Whenever it pelted or froze,
Till we showed him how feathers were proof against
    weathers ;
  With that he bethought him of hose.
And next it was plain that he in the rain
  Was forced to sit dripping and blind,
While the reed-warbler swung in a nest with her young,
  Deep-sheltered and warm from the wind.
So our homes in the boughs made him think of the house;
  And the swallow, to help him invent,
Revealed the best way to economise clay,
  And bricks to combine with cement.
The knowledge withal of the carpenter's awl
  Is drawn from the nuthatch's bill,
And the sand-marten's pains in the hazel-clad lanes
  Instructed the mason to drill.
Is there one of the arts more dear to men's hearts,
  To the birds' inspiration they owe it,

For the nightingale first sweet music rehearsed,
    Prima donna, composer, and poet.
The owl's dark retreats showed sages the sweets
    Of brooding to spin or unravel
Fine webs in one's brain, philosophical, vain,—
    The swallows the pleasures of travel,
Who chirped in such strain of Greece, Italy, Spain,
    And Egypt, that men, when they heard,
Were mad to fly forth from their nests in the north,
    And follow the tail of the bird.
Besides, it is true to our wisdom is due
    The knowledge of sciences all,
And chiefly those rare metaphysics of air
    Men Meteorology call.
For, indeed, it is said a kingfisher when dead
    Has his science alive in him still;
And, hung up, he will show how the wind means to
    blow,
    And turn to the point with his bill.*

---

* "A conceit supported chiefly by present practice, yet not made out by reason or experience."—Sir Thomas Browne, 'Vulgar Errors,' b. iii. c. 10. Oh, Sir Thomas! how had you the heart to touch it? If you had lived in the days of modern science you would have been more merciful to the humorous and the beautiful. Surely it was no *vulgar* error.

And men in their words acknowledge the birds'
　　Erudition in weather and star;
For they say, "'Twill be dry—the swallow is high;"
　　Or, "Rain—for the chough is afar."
'Twas the rooks who taught men vast pamphlets to pen
　　Upon Social Compact and Law,
And Parliaments hold, as themselves did of old,
　　Exclaiming "Hear, hear!" for "Caw, caw!"
When they build, if one steal, so great is their zeal
　　For justice, that all, at a pinch,
Without legal test will demolish his nest,
　　And hence is the trial by Lynch.
And whence arose love?　Go ask of the dove,
　　Or behold how the titmouse, unresting,
Still early and late ever sings by his mate,
　　To lighten her labours of nesting.
Their bonds never gall, though the leaves shoot and fall,
　　And the seasons roll round in their course,
For their Marriage each year grows more lovely and dear,
　　And they know not decrees of Divorce.
That these things are truth we have learned from our
　　　youth,
　　For our hearts to our customs incline,
As the rivers that roll from the fount of our soul,
　　Immortal, unchanging, divine.

Man, simple and old, in his ages of gold,
 Derived from our teaching true light,
And deemed it his praise in his ancestors' ways
 To govern his footsteps aright.
But the fountain of woes, Philosophy, rose,
 And what betwixt Reason and Whim,
He has splintered our rules into sections and schools,
 So the world is made bitter for him.
But the birds, since on earth they discovered the worth
 Of their souls, and resolved, with a vow,
No custom to change for a new or a strange,
 Have attained unto Paradise now.

BIRD OF PARADISE.

Now, silence in court !   Clerk, make your report !
 Bring the witnesses all of them in !
Let accusers appear !   You jury give ear !
 The trial is now to begin !

WINDBAG.

Magnificent sir, we by no means demur.
 But first, since you deprecate fury,
And allow us fair-play, in the time-honoured way
 Permit me to challenge the jury.

BIRD OF PARADISE.

Why, this is but fair.

WINDBAG.

Then, first, I declare
There's a bird from the Island of Mull
Whom I sooner would die than put up with.

BIRD OF PARADISE.

But why?

WINDBAG.

Why, who would be judged by a *gull?*

BIRD OF PARADISE.

Very good.   Strike him off.

WINDBAG.

Now I don't mean to scoff,
But the law of our land will not brook
That a parson (fie! fie!) civil causes should try;
I therefore object to the *rook.*

BIRD OF PARADISE.

Be it so.   And what next?

WINDBAG.

    If you will not be vexed,
I submit we are each of us Men,
And with both of our mights have opposed Woman's
    Rights,
    And therefore I fear Jenny Wren.

BIRD OF PARADISE.

Come, my feelings you touch; you're presuming too
    much.

WINDBAG.

There's only one more who must budge,
And he can't have the face to sit still in his place;
    For a blackcap can only be judge.

BIRD OF PARADISE.

Well, well!   Is this all?

WINDBAG.

    So please you.

BIRD OF PARADISE.

Then call four jury-birds more with all speed,
The cormorant, chough, robin, redpole.   Enough.
    And now let the trial proceed.

JACKDAW.

Caw, caw, caw, caw, caw!
Ye souls, who by Law
Desire to have justice
And vengeance, whose trust is
In this our Recorder,
By threes and by twos
Hop up, and in order
These wretches accuse!

WINDBAG.

Hold! this is most informal! I protest.
"Twas for one crime we underwent arrest;
Now you indict us on our whole amount;
You must proceed upon a single count.

BIRD OF PARADISE.

Silence! the court pursues its usual way.
Show up the Rook; he first shall have his say.

(Enter ROOK.)

ROOK.

Caw, caw! My lord, ere I became a soul,
And left my England for the happier Pole,

I loved mankind. I built upon the bough
Hard by his hall; in autumn by the plough
I in the fresh brown fragrant furrow ran,
Crowning his labours : this was all for Man.
For so a dainty to my crop most sweet
I found, the chaffer's grub, delicious meat !
Which on the seeds would greedily have fed,
But I indeed kept down the price of bread.
Then Man—ingratitude beyond belief !—
Calling me idler, vagabond, and thief,
Shot me, and left the saviour of his grain
To bleach and rot (malignant !) in the rain.
But hither came my soul (thrice happy bird !)—
This is the truth. I have my charge preferred.

BIRD OF PARADISE.

Well said ! and I believe you, by my beak !
But now hop off, and let the pigeon speak.

(Exit ROOK *; enter* PIGEON.)

PIGEON.

Even as the Rook, I wished this creature well ;
And ofttimes, flying from the leafless dell,

I upon ploughlands perched, and grassy meads,
Feeding in winter on the sweet small seeds:
For there I feared a too luxuriant yield
Might choke the springtide promise of the field;
Therefore I took a tithe, and man, to cap
The generous thought, repaid me with the trap.

(*Exit; enter* LARK.)

LARK.

I too, the herald of the day begun,
Who woke the ploughman's cock, who woke the sun—
I, child of brightness, spent a dark old age,
And died in foul Seven-Dials and a cage.

(*Exit; enter* GOLDFINCH.)

GOLDFINCH.

Why, hither I myself was sent to die,
Far from green leaves.

(*Exit; enter* BLACKBIRD.)

BLACKBIRD.

And I.

(*Exit; enter* THRUSH.)

THRUSH.

And I.

(*Exit; enter* LINNET.)

LINNET.

And I.

(*Exit; enter* GOOSE.)

GOOSE.

Protector of the birds, I vengeance claim
Against this fellow.

(*Hissing at* MARESNEST.)

BIRD OF PARADISE.

Wherefore, cackling dame?

GOOSE.

Among the geese it was accounted praise
To walk unswerving in their fathers' ways;
No mother was supposed to do amiss,
Who taught her goslings the ancestral hiss,
Commended precedent in laying eggs,
Or pressed a well-bred waddle of the legs.

These things, I say, were our established glories;
But when this *savant* rose, reviling Tories,
Our goslings at their sires began to sniff,
And called their ways inflexible and stiff.*

BIRD OF PARADISE.

Such high complaints from your own shores come
    forth;
Here too are pressing eiders from the north;
And western humming-birds, eye-dazzling clan;
Pied swallows too, complaining from Japan
Of nests dissolved in soup; and thousands more,
Small beaks, each twittering charges by the score.
But now, ye sons of men, lest time prove short,
Make some defence to this high-feathered court.

CHORUS.

Prodigious, we vow,
Are these charges, but now
Let us hear and take heed
What this poet will plead.

* "The goose seems to have a singularly inflexible organisation."—Darwin, 'Origin of Species,' c. 1.

He will speak from a mind
Bright, subtle, refined,
And he hopes by contention,
Or error, or quip,
Or by force of invention,
To give us the slip.

WINDBAG.

Immortal birds, I neither will nor can
Excuse all crimes, all cruelties of man.
But since to our account you mean to place
The debt of these the ill-doings of our race,
Now let their balance of good deeds be heard,
And learn what thanks man merits from the Bird.
For once we paid you honours as divine :
Witness the ibis raised to Egypt's shrine : *
And kings of old would swear ('tis dropt at present),
A form of oath, " By God and by the Pheasant ! "
Three times the traveller on lone waste-lands high
Stooped in obeisance to the single pie.
Grey storks in Amsterdam, time-honoured guests,
In antique tiles and chimneys built their nests,

* Herodotus, ii. 75.

And sojourned long, state-clients, reverent, mild,
While every father showed them to his child,
Praising their filial piety and fear;
So much did men the long-legged birds revere.
All lovers prized your worth : witness the Dove
Anacreon gave Bathyllus, pledge of love ; *
Women the most of all ; oft have you played
In the kind bosom of some mistress maid ;
And many a wife her parrot has adored
Even as her lapdog, and beyond her lord.
Speak to my truth, O Sparrow of Rome, twice blest !
For when you lived, it was in Lesbia's breast ;
And when you died, his verse Catullus lent,
And made you famous in a monument.
Besides, in winter, when stiff rime and ice
Closed in the worm, and froze the tender flies--

* Ἐρασμίη πέλεια,
  Πόθεν, πόθεν πετᾶσαι ;
  Πόθεν μύρων τοσούτων
  Ἐπ' ἠέρος θέουσα
  Πνέεις τε καὶ ψεκάζεις ;
  Τίς εἶ ; τί σοι μέλει δέ ;
  Ἀνακρέων μ' ἔπεμψεν,
  Πρὸς παῖδα, πρὸς Βάθυλλον,
  Τὸν ἄρτι τῶν ἀπάντων
  Κρατοῦντα καὶ τύραννον.
          —ANACREON.

When stript the holly stood, and bare the yew—
Then have I watched the small white-handed crew
Stand in the porch, and, scattering meal and crumb,
Bid all the hungry birds to breakfast come.
You, too, the tongues of poets in all times
Have wooed in woodlands with their honeyed rhymes
Paying you worship ; and beyond all these
The merry Greek, sweet Aristophanes.
O happy souls ! who once in Athens heard
The laughing city deify the Bird !

CHORUS.

O thou to whom on the sun-bright mountains
　We chirped and chattered within the yew,
Or on red fruits falling by orchard fountains,
　Fresh, well watered with rain and dew !
Oh ! how oft hast thou heard Ilissus' meadows
　Of olives quiver with morning tune !
Or the nightingale's notes through the garden shadows
　Ring on the river beneath the moon !

To thee, to thee, our pupil, our poet,
　When life had its pleasures, when man was young,
We opened our heart that thou mightst know it,
　Taught thee our measures, revealed our tongue.

And we know in the world thy melody lingers;
  While men dwell in it, it shall not cease ;
O dearest, sweetest of beakless singers !
  Friend of the linnet ! glory of Greece !

WINDBAG.

If man's good work may cancel man's ill deed,
For us let English Chaucer intercede.
Think with what rhymes, what measures old and quaint,
He sings your love-day, and exalts your saint !
Think how he rose from bed betimes in spring,
To hear the nightingale and cuckoo sing !

NIGHTINGALE.

O flower of the prime ! O fountain of rhyme !
  O lover of daisies ! O poet of May !
Thy boon and my debt if I ever forget,
  Let my heart have forgotten her lay.

Thou didst drive from my view "the lewd cuckoo ;"
  And I was thy singer that whole May long.*

* " And then y-came the nightingale to me,
    And sayid, ' Frende, forsoth I thanké thee

Time since has grown grey, but I love thee to-day,
  And I solace my soul with thy song.

WINDBAG.

Yet one last name, O Birds, I will engage
In our behalf. Remember Selborne's sage !
How oft have ye beheld his footsteps crown
Your leafy hanger, or your open down,
Or strayed sometimes where the dwarf oak-tree veins
With crooked and sprawling roots your sandstone lanes !
He, bright historian of your loves and feuds,
Dated your building, chronicled your broods,
Described your times of flight, your change of feathers,
Your light moods shifted with the shifting weathers,
And, by long commerce with his gable guests,
Learned all the secrets of your souls and nests.
Chiefly to you I plead, whose airy host,
And manifold migrations pleased him most.
How strained his eye for that first April comer,
Promise of old companions and the summer !

> That thou hast likid me for to rescowe
> And avowe to Love y-make I now,
> That all this Maie I woll they singir be."
>   —CHAUCER : "The Cuckowe and the Nightingale."

How pensive watched your "placid easy flight" *
Southwards! Ye swallows, think of Gilbert White!

SWALLOW.

If Transmigration e'er compel
    A bird to live with human heart,
I pray that bird have choice to dwell
    From human ills apart.

When swallows through the world went forth,
    And watched affairs in every nation,
They found for ever, south and north,
    Vanity and Vexation.

So let him dwell not in the Town—
    There Trade and Penury roar and weep:

---

* The reader will forgive me the length of the following exquisite
extract : " If ever I saw anything like actual migration, it was last
Michaelmas Day.   I was travelling, and out early in the morning:
at first there was a vast fog ; but by the time that I was got seven
or eight miles from home towards the coast, the sun broke out into
a delicate warm day.   We were then on a large heath or common,
and I could discern, as the mist began to break away, great num-
bers of swallows clustering on the stunted shrubs and bushes, as if
they had roosted there all night.   As soon as the air became clear
and pleasant they were all on the wing at once, and by a placid
easy flight proceeded on southwards towards the sea : after this I
did not see any more flocks, only now and then a straggler."—
White's ' History of Selborne.'

But 'neath the silence of a down
  Disturbed by grazing sheep.

There, like his brook, his life shall glide,
  Far from State-party, plot, and treason,
Nor feel the flow of Fortune's tide,
  Beyond the change of season.

There he shall Learning woo, and Art,
  Without a rival to unthrone;
Nor seek to pain another's heart,
  Since he may please his own.

Books he shall read in hill and tree;
  The flowers his weather shall portend
The birds his moralists shall be;
  And everything his friend.

Such man in England I have seen;
  He moved my heart with fresh delight;
And had I not the swallow been,
  I had been Gilbert White.

WINDBAG.

I say no more : you have heard all my case :
Let these your friends plead for our guilty race :
And I myself—if now despite my crimes
You set me free—will pay you with sweet rhymes,
Praising your beaks and claws, and in high words
I will exalt the Paradise of Birds.

BIRD OF PARADISE.

Nay, you remind me now of Æsop's crane,
Who, when the farmer caught him in his grain,
Swore by his feathers, if he met with grace,
He would warn all his neighbours off the place.
Yet I confess you have not pleaded ill ;
And by my beak ! I'd vote for no true bill :
But Law is Law ; our likings must not force
Our statutes ; no—the Law must take its course.

WINDBAG.

So fond of Law !   Why, then, you must admit
You can by Law do nothing but acquit.
Your law, discovering a most clear intention
Respecting souls, of bodies makes no mention.

That we have bodies, though we've reached the Pole,
Is plain, which you must kill to find the soul.
But 'tis as clear that, if you do this deed,
You will the limits of your Law exceed.

BIRD OF PARADISE (*to* JACKDAW).

Is this the truth?

JACKDAW.

Yes, as the statutes go.

BIRD OF PARADISE.

Is there no word about a body?

JACKDAW.

No.

BIRD OF PARADISE.

Nor any precedent, if this were done,
Which might excuse us to the Birds?

JACKDAW.

Not one.

BIRD OF PARADISE.

They both are guilty.

JACKDAW.

'Tis more clear than day.

BIRD OF PARADISE.

But there's no way to find them so?

JACKDAW.

No way.

BIRD OF PARADISE.

Then they must be discharged.   A legal flaw
Is (blest be Justice!) stronger than the Law.
You are not guilty, therefore you are free ;
And thank for this the Birds' great clemency.
Sparrows, stand off!   And now that you are loose,
You may make explanation and excuse,
Not to be heard in court :—say more at large
Wha brings you here, your embassy, and charge.

WINDBAG.

But first receive these presents that we bear,
A sweet confection delicate and rare ;

For when she sent us here 'twas England's wish
To find your royal beak some dainty dish.
> (*Offers him a cockchafer of great size.*)

BIRD OF PARADISE (*eating*).

O food of Paradise ! divine repast !
Sweeter than hawberries or beechen mast !
Beyond all insects grateful to my bill,
Ants of Peru, or beetles of Brazil !
O thou, who must be cook to mightiest kings,
Come, that I may embrace thee with my wings !
Say how the woods of England now produce
Such insects, vast beyond all former use ;
For not on western leaves or tropic mould
Did I so great a beetle once behold.

WINDBAG.

And yet of mightier shapes our land is full,
Whose boom is like the bellow of a bull,
And like a stag their horns ; nay, sometimes one
Will with his outspread wings eclipse the sun :
But slow of flight, and so an easy prey ;
How sweet their flavour is your crop can say.

Now, when they saw these wondrous wingèd breeds,
Mankind, remorseful for their old ill-deeds,
Bade us ambassadors to Birdland come,
And tidings bring of your Millennium ;
And if you grant what our memorial begs,
Each of your kinds will lay for us two eggs,
Which we, embarking on the Polar foam,
Will carry south, and have them hatched at home.
Lo ! what a prospect for your children's bills !
What airy chase on their ancestral hills !
What regal honours to their race assigned !
Their maintenance beetles, and their slaves mankind !

BIRD OF PARADISE.

Man of honeyed words,
O persuasive poet !
Mention to the Birds—
For they first must know it--
If their sons return
To your hills and hedges,
What things they will earn
By way of privileges.

WINDBAG.

Upon every tree,
Royal feathered martyr,
There shall surely be
Graven a great Charter,
Wherein all may read
Upon what a basis
Men and Birds agreed
To live as brother races.
Save by your free-will,
None shall touch or taste ye,
Roast you, fry, or grill,
Or crowd you in a pasty.
No man e'er shall get
A reprieve or pardon,
Who shall dare to net
Or shoot you in his garden :
But to you we will allot
Acres of wild cherry,
And walls of apricot,
And fig-trees to make merry.
When your nesting is begun,
Whatever truant urchin

Take more eggs than one
Shall receive a birching.
But men in woodland rooms
Shall build you aviaries,
To keep the blackbirds' plumes
As dry as tame canaries.
And in them we will shape
Gold and silver cages,
With hemp-seed and sweet rape,
Where, in your pilgrimages,
You may fly in to eat ;
And little crystal vessels,
Full of waters sweet,
Hung on mossy trestles.
And there in spring shall come
Crowds of wingless mortals,
Bringing their humble dumb
Petitions to your portals.
For instance, if a girl
Wish a new hat or bonnet,
She must a leaflet curl,
And write discreetly on it,
" When you moult your blue
Feathers, great Kingfisher,

Save a plume or two
For your own well-wisher."
Sparrows, we will keep
In the chimney pen your
Nests, and not a sweep
Shall disturb the tenure.
Unto all birds too
Honours long to mention
Shall be paid if you
Make this great Convention.

BIRD OF PARADISE.

Birds, will you agree
To oblige these strangers?
Shall our children be
Once more woodland rangers?
Ho, then ! great white owls,
Go, your parks repeople !
Sparrows to your cowls !
Jackdaws to the steeple !
You who in the furze
Lodge by hillside burrows,
Or pipe o'er gossamers
In the autumn furrows ;

You that nest in corn,
Or build amid the hedges,
With the bittern on the bourne
Or with the coot in sedges ;
Birds of single note,
Birds who pipe and whistle,
Blackbird, lark, whitethroat,
Thrushes, song and missel ;
Spirits of the North,
Bring your eggs together !
We will send them forth
To English hedge or heather.
Now let such eggs be laid
As will exalt the nation ;
For the birds with men have made
A reconciliation.

CHORUS.

O men, ye life-tenants of earth and of ocean !
    Say why did you grudge the bright kingdoms of air
To the Birds who partook of your human devotion,
    Your twins in thanksgiving, your partners in prayer ?

On high-days of old we have seen you assemble,
    Wise counsel and gifts from your gods to bespeak ;
We have heard from our nests in the roofs of the temple
    Your low supplications, the Lydian, the Greek.

It is told, it is told how the voice of Apollo
    Rolled forth in his thunder, affrighting the thieves,
When they plundered the nest of his suppliant the swallow,
    Who sought his asylum, and built in his eaves.*

Moreover ye know by what toilsome endeavour
    The beak of the crossbill was twisted awry,
And since what Oblation the robin for ever
    Has red on his bosom in winter, and why.

The Birds had a share in your earthly dominions ;
    Ye sailed the same waters we crossed on the wing ;
Ye breathed of our air, and the flash of our pinions
    Advised you of autumn, and chronicled spring.

* "'Thereupon Aristodicus adopted the following expedient
He went round the temple and removed the sparrows, and all the
other kinds of birds that nested in the temple.   And while he was
thus employed it is said that a voice issued from the shrine in the
direction of Aristodicus, saying, ' Most sacrilegious of men ! how
darest thou do this? art thou destroying my suppliants from my
temple ?' "—Herodotus, i. 159.

One source of delight and one fountain of sorrow
    Replenished the rivers in both of our breasts;
To-day we were merry, and death on the morrow
    Found Man in his roof-tree, the Birds in their nests.

If Heaven accepted our joint adoration,
    If Earth was to both an abode and a tomb,
Why could we not sojourn, O Man, as one nation?
    Were waste-lands so precious? had mountains no
        room?

Or were ye so wingless, so wanting in vision,
    Ye saw not as we did the things of the sky,
But dooming the Birds to your earthly ambition,
    Forgot in vainglory yourselves were to die?
        (Birds are seen approaching in the air, car-
        rying nests full of eggs in their beaks.)

WINDBAG.

O rare! O wonder! O delight!
See, Maresnest, see! the prettiest sight!
The Birds in kind have each obeyed
The Monarch, and their eggs have laid.
Now they fly hither two and two,
The nightingale, the plain cuckoo,

THE PARADISE OF BIRDS.

The jay in crimson clad and blue,
Robin in scarlet livery seen,
And woodpecker in Lincoln green,
And martin with white satin vest,
And peewit proud of soldier crest,
Blackcap with eye in merry mood
Twinkling beneath his velvet hood,
And jackdaw with his sable mate,
But grey and reverent both in pate;
Besides all kinds of beak and wing,
That walk, and hop, and fly, and sing.
Within their beaks round nests they bear
One on each side, aloft in air,
Compact of softest moss and wool,
Well-wov'n and warm, of eggs brimful—
Beautiful eggs, oval, and bright
In the green shell, or smooth and white,
Like opals clear against the light,
Or blue as skies that summer crown,
Or toned to modest russet brown,
Or else to olive verging more,
And with dark mottling dappled o'er,
But delicately as might twin
Soft freckles on a woman's skin.

In orderly procession straight,
They seek our iceberg with their freight.
Come, turn we there ourselves, and stow
The cargo safe—then southward ho !

(*The Birds deposit the nests at the gate
of Limbo.* MARESNEST *and* WINDBAG
convey the nests through the ROC'S *Egg,
and arrange them on the iceberg. The*
CHORUS *seat themselves on the top of
the Egg, the* BIRD OF PARADISE *in
their midst.*)

BIRD OF PARADISE.

Set safe your stores ; embosom well
Each nest, and bury every shell.
First spread soft wool, then depths of down,
And both with hardy lichens crown ;
Lest ere they reach the kindly coast
The searching unfamiliar frost
Pierce through the crevices, and freeze
Some tender life upon the seas.

WINDBAG.

For this, for all, thanks, gentle Birds !
Well will we keep our plighted words.
Maresnest, the reins !   Go quick ! set free
The Bears !   Once more we are at sea !
Our dreams found true, our errand done !
And now for England and the sun !

(*They put to sea.*)

CHORUS.

Go from the home of your birth,
   Children unhatched in the shell !
Go afar off upon earth,
   In the woods of your fathers to dwell !
To pair in your leafy possessions,
   To mingle, in sunlight or shade,
Your labours, your loves, and your sessions,
   Your lingering late serenade !

Snow-wingèd, wave-loving hosts,
   Whiten the skirts of the land !
Pipe on the summer-clad coasts,
   Warming your bosoms in sand !

Build high on the piles of the granite,
  And over calm fisheries float,
From the Longships far eastward to Thanet,
  The Lizard to lone John o' Groat!

You, too, swallows, that hatch
  Broods by the dwellings of men,
Colonise chimney and thatch,
  Fresh from migration again!
Shoot swift over market and haven,
  Or gnat-haunted river, that hems
Grass meadows, serene-flowing Avon,
  The aits and the willows of Thames!

Eremite birds and recluse,
  Lovers of infinite room,
Go, for your tenements choose
  Cromlech, and sheepway, and combe!
The curlew once more in the fallow
  Shall whistle at night by the main;
The peewit, whose children are callow,
  Lament upon Salisbury Plain.

Rivers and streams shall resound;
  The water-rat down in the reeds

THE PARADISE OF BIRDS.

Shall hear the sedge-warbler around,
  And the crake on the low-lying meads :
And the bittern shall boom o'er the rushes
  Love-signals deep-throated and harsh,
Where solitude mournfully hushes
  The stagnated pools of the marsh.

Yet, wheresoe'er ye shall roam,
  Seek not in life for your goal ;
Death shall restore you your home,
  Death the imparadised Pole.
Then mingle with melody Reason,
  And if, upon mountain or glen,
Ye sing of the change of the season,
  Say this to the children of Men :—

In the spring-time, chaffinch gay,—
  " Vanished is the winter snow ;
Days grow longer" (you shall say) ;
  " Apple-blossoms soon will blow.
Haste, ye wingless lovers, then,
  Take your pleasures ere 'tis late
Birds are building, maids and men,
  Every one selects his mate.

Now St Valentine is past,
    April will in time be May;
Youth that lingers will not last;
    There's a sunset every day.
Birds and poets both have sung
Love comes only to the young."

Sing, O nightingale, in June:
    " Now it is the shortest night,
And to-morrow's sun by noon
    Will have climbed his yearly height.
Rarer sounds the blackbird's pipe;
    Redder glows the apricot;
Everything is still and ripe;
    From to-morrow all things rot.
Life's climacteric of power
    Is the half-way house of Death;
Man's decline, like bird and flower,
    Dates from parting of a breath.
Night must now shift hands with day;
Fullest ripeness brings decay."

Swallow, in September sing:
    "Quit we now our northern eaves;

All the gnats are perishing ;
    Sere and sapless look the leaves.
Where are flown the summer flies?
    Like men's riches they have wings.
Vanity of vanities !
    Fleeting are all feathered things !
We have read our horoscope,
    But in summer we forget ;
Every spring awakes new hope,
    Every autumn new regret.
'Tis the truth (but truth is strange),
Nought's immutable but Change."

Snow-bunting in winter cry :
    " Misery, and cold, and dearth !
Darkness in the shrouded sky !
    Silence o'er the snowy earth !
Every tree looks white and wan,
    Barbed with icicles, unclad,
Like some featherless old man,
    Withered, toothless, poor, and sad.
Yet be trustful, Man and Bird ;
    Winter shall not kill the soul.

I

Life on earth is hope deferred,
  Since beyond it lies the Pole.
Death, whose bounds are snow and ice,
Is the door of Paradise."

MARESNEST.

Adieu! O chattering birds, say what you will,
I, for my part, shall keep my theory still.

(*Exeunt.*)

THE END.

PRINTED BY WILLIAM BLACKWOOD AND SONS, EDINBURGH.

www.ingramcontent.com/pod-product-compliance
Lightning Source LLC
Chambersburg PA
CBHW030906050726
47500CB00009B/1133